LARGE PRINT

Animal
Stories

Brown Watson
ENGLAND

Shawna the Sheep

Farmer Nancy was proud of her sheep. Their wool was the finest that anyone had ever seen. The sheep with the best wool was Shawna. 'My wool is so soft!' she kept saying. 'People only come to Farmer Nancy to buy wool because I am here!'

One day, Shawna saw a lady and a man looking at all the other sheep in the meadow. Farmer Nancy was there too. 'Shawna!' she cried. 'I was just coming to find you!'

'Meet Kate and Bill!' said Farmer Nancy.
'They are going to spin wool this year at the summer fair!'
'And it is your wool we want to spin!' said Bill. 'Such fine, soft wool!'

This made Shawna feel very proud! Off she went in a smart trailer with Farmer Nancy, looking very grand! The day was fine and warm and she felt rather hot. But that did not matter!

There was a crowd waiting to see Shawna at the fair! Farmer Nancy took some wisps of wool from her fleece and Bill spun them into a long thread on his spinning wheel.

'This wool will be made into a lovely, soft scarf!' Kate told the crowd. 'It is the finest, softest wool that anyone can buy!' After that, everyone wanted to pet Shawna and feel her wool.

Shawna soon felt very hot indeed! But she tried not to mind. 'You are quite a famous sheep, Shawna!' said Farmer Nancy. 'But I am sure you will be glad when shearing begins tomorrow!'

'What is shearing?' said Shawna. But Farmer Nancy did not hear. Shawna had to wait until she was back at the farm. She went to see the other sheep.
'What is shearing?' she asked them.

'It's when you feel cooler!' said one.
'And lighter!' said another.
'And smaller!' added a third sheep.
'Cooler?' bleated Shawna. 'Lighter?
Smaller? But, what IS shearing?'

'Don't you know?' another sheep bleated
back. 'Shearing is when you lose your
thick, woolly coat!'
And off they went, bleating in delight at the
look of shock on Shawna's face.

'N-no!' she cried. 'Not my lovely, soft wool?' But it was true. Next day, the shearers were busy peeling away the wool from each sheep. How bare they all looked afterwards!

They skipped and jumped around, feeling so light and so cool in the warm sunshine! But Shawna's mouth was wide open in horror. She did not want to lose her soft, fine wool!

Off she ran, feeling so very hot! She was glad to rest in the shade of a big tree. But, as the sun rose higher, the shadow of the tree became shorter, until there was no shade at all!

Feeling even hotter, Shawna ran into the dairy, where butter and cheese were made. There were tiles on the walls and on the floor, smooth and cool. Shawna began to feel better.

Then, a strong hand pushed her from behind. 'Out you go, Shawna!' said the dairyman. 'Today is shearing day! Time to lose your woolly coat!' And he pushed her out of the door!

Off she ran again until she came to a stream. Shawna put her feet into the cool water. 'That is better!' she said. 'I was feeling SO hot!' Still the sun beat down on her woolly back.

Then Shawna had another shock. It was Sam, the sheep-dog! 'Woof! Woof!' he barked. 'So here you are, Shawna! Farmer Nancy says you must come and get sheared!'

'I WILL not lose my fine, soft wool!' bleated Shawna. 'I will NOT!' And off she ran. But Sam could run faster. He darted in front, so that she could go no further. Then Shawna had an idea.

There was a wire fence around the field. Shawna began to squeeze under it. Sam, the sheep-dog, could not follow her now! Suddenly, she felt a strong tug at her coat.

'Baa!' bleated Shawna. Had Sam taken hold of her wool in his strong teeth? She tried to pull free.

'Woof!' barked Sam. 'You have caught your coat on the wire, Shawna!'

Sam ran to fetch Farmer Nancy. 'Hold still, Shawna!' she said. 'I must cut you free. Then you can come and have your fleece sheared properly! You silly sheep!'

By now, Shawna was too tired and much too hot to do anything! All the other sheep were skipping about and enjoying the sunshine without their thick woolly coats.

The shearer soon cut away Shawna's fine, soft wool! 'It's a shame about the big hole in your fleece,' he said. 'That is where you caught your wool on the wire fence!' Poor Shawna!

But, she had to admit, she did feel very nice and cool! Then, Bill spun lots of woolly thread on his spinning wheel, ready for Kate to weave into beautiful scarves and shawls!

Their work won first prize at the town craft fair! 'Fine, soft sheep's wool makes beautiful things,' said Kate. And Shawna, standing in her pen beside Farmer Nancy, quite agreed!

Ben and Rosy

Ben and Rosy were two big, strong horses. They had worked at Hill Farm for a long, long time. 'Your Grandad had Ben and Rosy when I was a boy,' Farmer West told his children, Jack and Susan. 'Hill Farm would not be quite the same without them!'

'But,' he went on, 'they are getting old and they are getting slow. I think it is time that we made some changes at Hill Farm!'
Jack and Susan looked at each other. What did their dad mean?

They soon found out! One morning there came a loud 'BEEP! BEEP!' and two big, black wheels and something shiny and red appeared! 'Dad has bought a tractor!' shouted Susan.

'And Mum is driving it!' added Jack. They stopped feeding the chickens and went to get a closer look. Mum and Dad looked very pleased. The tractor looked so bright and cheerful!

'Meet Toby the tractor!' Mum said. 'He can pull a plough, clear a ditch, tow a trailer, move heavy loads...'
'But Ben and Rosy do all that!' said Susan. 'What work will they do?'

'They can have a rest!' said Dad. 'The tractor can do their work in half the time!' That was true. With the tractor it was possible to plough a field, dig a ditch and put up a fence in one day!

And the tractor still looked bright and cheerful, not at all tired!
'Good old Toby the tractor!' said the farmer.
He even gave the tractor's front wheel a pat, just like he used to pat Ben and Rosy!

'It seems very strange for us not to be working on the farm,' Ben said to Rosy. 'I do not like it,' Rosy said to Ben. 'With no work for us to do, there is no need for the farmer to keep us here!'

'No need to talk like that!' said Ben. 'Toby
the tractor cannot do everything!'
But Rosy shook her big head sadly.
'It seems to me,' she said, 'there is nothing
that tractor cannot do!'

This time, Ben said nothing. He had a horrible feeling that Rosy might be right. How long would the farmer be able to let them stay if the tractor was doing their work?

Ben lifted his big head up to the sky.
'Let us go into our stable,' he said. 'It looks
like rain.' Rosy stamped her big hooves.
She tried not to look at Farmer West
working with the tractor again.

'That is all the planting done!' he called to his wife. 'Just in time before a spell of bad weather, too! And it's all thanks to our new tractor!' He just managed to lock up the shed as rain began to fall.

It rained all night long. Ben and Rosy heard it beating down on the roof of their stable. Early next day, the door opened and in came Jack and Susan in their rainhats and wellington boots.

'Hello, Ben and Rosy,' said Jack.
'Here are your oats and some hay,' said Susan. But before Ben and Rosy had begun to eat, there came a loud cry from the yard outside.

'Come along, Toby!' cried Farmer West.
'We have work to do! The rain has washed
away so much soil from Bottom Field that
our new fence has started to fall down! It is
sliding into the stream!'

Then came the sound of the tractor starting up. Jack and Susan left Ben and Rosy in the stable and ran to see what was happening. The rain had made the ground muddy and slippery.

But Toby the tractor looked as bright and as cheerful as ever! By the time Jack and Susan reached Bottom Field, he was already lifting the pieces of fence out of the stream!

Each piece was loaded carefully into the farm trailer. Then, Farmer West hooked the trailer to the back of the tractor. Everyone looked very pleased. Jack and Susan felt like cheering!

Then, Farmer West got back into the driving seat and started up the engine. Toby the tractor made a lot of noise as he tried to pull the heavy trailer. His wheels spun round in the muddy ground.

Toby tried to go forwards, but he could not move! The more his wheels spun round, the deeper he sank into the mud. 'Drat!' cried Farmer West. 'Now, what can we do?'

Just then there came the sound of plodding hooves from the old stables.

'Ben and Rosy!' cried Susan.

'Ben and Rosy!' cried Jack. 'They can pull the tractor out of the mud!'

Ben and Rosy were led to Bottom Field. Soon, their big strong hooves were plodding slowly across the soggy, muddy ground as they made their way towards Toby the tractor.

They could see that Toby was very pleased to see them! Farmer West worked quickly to fasten their harness firmly to the front of the tractor. 'Over to you, Ben and Rosy!' he said. 'Pull!'

Ben and Rosy pulled hard. In no time at all, they had pulled the tractor, the heavy trailer and all the pieces of fencing out of the muddy ground and onto dry land!

This time, Jack and Susan really did cheer! 'Good old Ben and Rosy! We still need them to work on our farm!' Toby winked his headlights to show that he quite agreed.

Daisy Donkey

Daisy Donkey was not at all dainty. She was big and clumsy, with bald patches on her coat. She had been called Daisy by Ken, a man at the animal shelter. 'Daisy has been badly treated,' he told Farmer Green.

'Could your Tom and Katie look after her?'
'Please, Dad!' cried Tom.
'Please!' added Katie. 'Daisy really needs a good home!'
Farmer Green nodded. 'She can stay on our farm,' he said. 'You can look after her!'

Tom and Katie were very glad! Daisy loved being on the farm. She would wait by the gate for them to get home from school. Then she would bend her head for them to scratch her long ears.

But she jumped at the slightest sound! If one of the farm dogs barked, or the cockerel crowed, or if a noisy lorry went past, Daisy would bray in fright! 'Hee-Haw! HEE-HAW!'

'No need to be frightened,' said Katie. She
stroked Daisy along her back.
'Daisy was frightened by something which
made a loud noise,' said Ken. 'She cannot
forget it.'

The days became longer. Katie and Tom found a rug, a bridle and a saddle for Daisy. They put on riding hats and took turns to ride the little donkey and lead her around the meadow.

'It is lucky that Daisy came to your farm,'
Ken said. 'Our shelter was too small for her
to stay for long.'
'Can't you make the animal shelter bigger?'
asked Katie.

'We cannot afford it!' said Ken. 'But we are hoping to make some money at the Town Show next Saturday! Will you come and buy something from our stall?'

Help Ferndale
Animal Shelter
at the
Town Show

'You know we will!' said Katie. 'But I do
wish we could help some more!'
'So do I,' said Tom. They both began to
think hard. Daisy wanted to help too,
nuzzling them with her long nose.

'I know!' said Katie at last. 'Let's wear
some big posters saying – PLEASE HELP
THE ANIMAL SHELTER – and take Daisy
to the show! She can carry a tin to collect
the money!'

Tom and Katie worked hard, drawing and painting the posters. Then, two posters were threaded on string, so that one poster would be at the front and the other at the back.

Farmer Green hung a collecting tin
carefully around Daisy's neck. 'Put on
your riding hat, Tom,' he said. 'You
can ride Daisy to the show with Katie
leading her!'

Daisy felt pleased with herself, and very proud. All along the way to the show, people came up and stroked and patted her, wanting to know about the animal shelter.

They put money in the collecting tin, too!
'Hee-haw!' cried Daisy each time a coin
clattered into the tin. Katie held the leading
rein firmly. 'It is all right, Daisy,' said Tom.
'It is all right.'

Children were blowing up balloons and making them go pop! 'Hee-Haw!' brayed Daisy in fright. Then a drum sounded. 'Boom-BOOM!' 'HEE-HAW!' went Daisy, louder still.

A line of horses with bells and ribbons went past Daisy. CRACK! Their trainer cracked her whip on the ground. She was telling the horses to turn a corner. CRACK! CRACK!

'HEE-HAW!' Daisy had never brayed quite so loudly. 'HEE-HAW! HEE-HAW!' She began to trot and then to run and then to gallop! 'Stop, Daisy!' shouted Tom. 'Please, stop!'

'Hee-haw! HEE-HAW!' It seemed to Tom that lots of other donkeys were joining in! He held on to Daisy with all his might! He wanted to shut his eyes tight, hardly daring to look up.

'Stop, young man!' someone shouted. 'You can stop now!'

'Hurrah!' someone else shouted. 'It's the donkey from the animal shelter! The one we saw on the road!'

Tom felt a strong arm around his back. A hand pulled gently at Daisy's bridle and Ken's calm voice spoke into her long ears. 'It's all right, Daisy. 'It's all right!'

Tom looked up at last, not feeling at all happy. 'I am sorry, Ken,' he began. 'We wanted to raise some money for the animal shelter, but...'
'And so you have!' Ken told him.

He gave a grin and waved a handful of money at Tom. 'Look! First prize for winning the Donkey Derby! And people are still giving us money! You and Daisy have done us proud!'